Florrie's Flag

It was a lovely sunny day in Fimble Valley.

Florrie was helping Baby Pom
to build a tower,
and Fimbo and Rockit
were having races.

Just as Florrie put the last block on the top of Baby Pom's tower, she heard the Tinkling Tree tinkling.

"I'm getting the Fimbling Feeling!" she cried.

"I can feel a twinkling,
I can hear a sound,
It's telling me there's something
Waiting to be found!
Where is it? Where is it?
What could it be?
I think it might be over there,
Let's go and see!"

Florrie's find looked like a black and white tablecloth stuck to a stick. She waved it in the air. Swoosh! Swoosh!

"Oooh, you've found a flag!" chirped Bessie. "A special flag! It's called a chequered flag. You wave it to finish a race."

"Fimbo and Rockit love races," said Florrie. "I'll go and wave my flag for them!"

All the racing they had done, though, had made Rockit and Fimbo very hungry.

And then all the apples and Crumble Crackers they had eaten had made them very sleepy...

Zzzzzzzzzzz...

"Fimbo, Rockit, wake up! Look what I've found!"
cried Florrie. "A special flag you use to finish a race."

"Fimbo! Glung! Want to race?" said Rockit.

Zzzzzzzzzz...

"Never mind!" said Rockit. "I'll race Bessie and Roly instead."

"We'll start and finish the race here, by Pom's tower," said Florrie.

"I'm just going to go and eat an apple to give me lots of energy," said Rockit, bouncing off.

"You start without me. I'm so fast, I'll easily catch up with Bessie and Roly!"

"Go Roly!" shouted Baby Pom.

"Go Bessie!" shouted Florrie.

But what had happened to Rockit?

Eating an apple had made Rockit sleepy all over again.

Zzzzzzzzzzz...

Baby Pom and Florrie's shouting
woke Rockit up.

"Glung!" he glunged, bouncing off the Comfy Corner.
"Oh no! The race!"

Rockit bounced as
fast as he could
past the Bubble Fall.

He bounced past
the Playdips.

He bounced past the
Tinkling Tree.

He bounced as he had never
bounced before.

At the finish line, Florrie was holding her flag.

Bessie fluttered past.

"Bessie's first," she cried. Swoosh! went the flag.

Roly rolled past.
"Roly's second," she cried. Swoosh!

Rockit bounced in at
     top speed...

...straight into Baby Pom's tower. CRASH!

"Rockit's third!" Florrie laughed. Swoosh!

"Tickle my tadpoles! That was fun, even though I didn't win!" said Rockit.

"What's going on?" yawned Fimbo, "I'm ready for more races now. Anyone want to race?"

"Yes!" shouted everyone.
Swoosh! went Florrie's flag.